Beatrix Potter's COUNTRY WORLD

The BEATRIX POTTER VISITORS BOOK

F. WARNE & Co

FREDERICK WARNE

Published by the Penguin Group
27 Wrights Lane, London W8 5TZ, England
Viking Penguin Inc., 40 West 23rd Street, New York, New York 10010, USA
Penguin Books Australia Ltd, Ringwood, Victoria, Australia
Penguin Books Canada Ltd, 2801 John Street, Markham, Ontario, Canada L3R 1B4
Penguin Books (NZ) Ltd, 182-190 Wairau Road, Auckland 10, New Zealand

Penguin Books Ltd, Registered Offices: Harmondsworth, Middlesex, England

First published 1989

1 3 5 7 9 10 8 6 4 2

ISBN 0 7232 3588 0

Printed and bound in Great Britain by
William Clowes Limited, Beccles and London

This Visitors Book
records visitors to the home of

____

____

____

Between ________________________

and __________________________

Date	*Name*	*Address*

Date	*Name*	*Address*

Date	Name	Address

Date	*Name*	*Address*

Date	Name	Address

Date	*Name*	*Address*

Date	Name	Address

Date	Name	Address

Date	Name	Address

Date	Name	Address

Date	*Name*	*Address*

Date	*Name*	*Address*

Date	*Name*	*Address*

Date	Name	Address

Date	Name	Address

Date	*Name*	*Address*

Date	Name	Address

Date	*Name*	*Address*

Date	Name	Address

Date	*Name*	*Address*

Date	Name	Address

Date	Name	Address

Date	*Name*	*Address*

Date	Name	Address

Date	*Name*	*Address*

Date	*Name*	*Address*

Date	Name	Address

Date	*Name*	*Address*

Date	*Name*	*Address*

Date	*Name*	*Address*

Date	Name	Address

Date	*Name*	*Address*

Date	Name	Address

Date	*Name*	*Address*

Date	*Name*	*Address*

Date	*Name*	*Address*

Date	*Name*	*Address*

Date	*Name*	*Address*

Date	*Name*	*Address*

Date	Name	Address

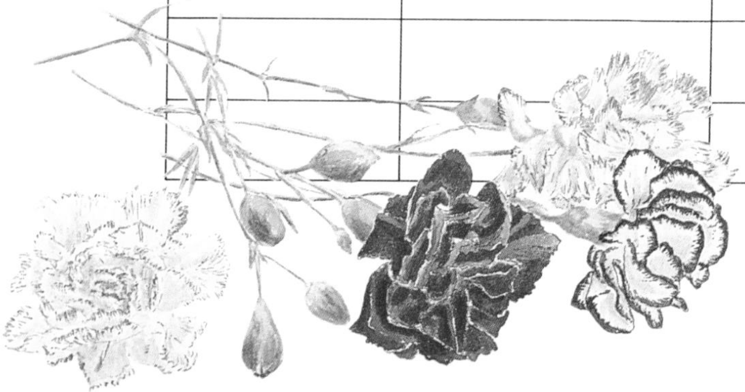

Date	Name	Address

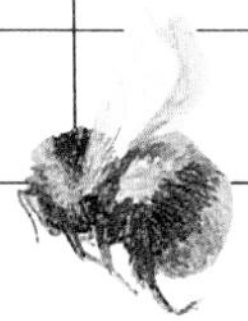

Date	Name	Address

Date	*Name*	*Address*

Date	*Name*	*Address*

Date	*Name*	*Address*

Date	Name	Address

Date	*Name*	*Address*

Date	*Name*	*Address*

Date	Name	Address

Date	*Name*	*Address*

Date	*Name*	*Address*

Date	*Name*	*Address*

Date	*Name*	*Address*

Date	Name	Address

Date	Name	Address

Date	*Name*	*Address*

Date	Name	Address

Date	Name	Address

Date	*Name*	*Address*

Date	*Name*	*Address*

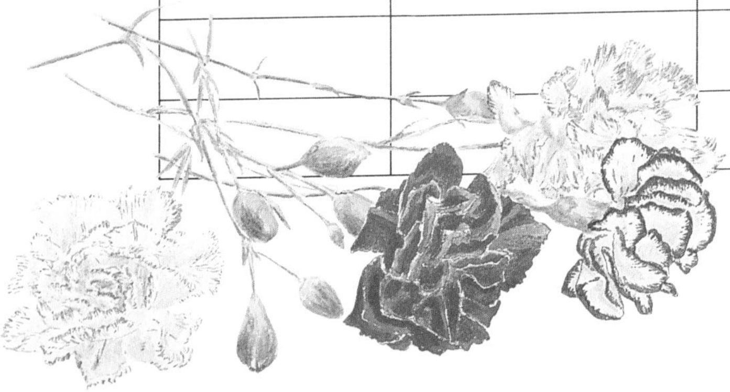

Date	*Name*	*Address*

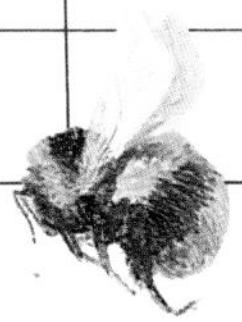

Date	Name	Address

Date	Name	Address

Date	Name	Address

Date	*Name*	*Address*

Date	*Name*	*Address*

Date	Name	Address

Date	Name	Address

Date	*Name*	*Address*

Date	*Name*	*Address*

Date	Name	Address

Date	Name	Address

Date	*Name*	*Address*

Date	Name	Address

Date	Name	Address

Date	Name	Address

Date	Name	Address

Date	Name	Address

Date	*Name*	*Address*

Date	*Name*	*Address*

Date	Name	Address

Date	Name	Address

Date	Name	Address

Date	Name	Address

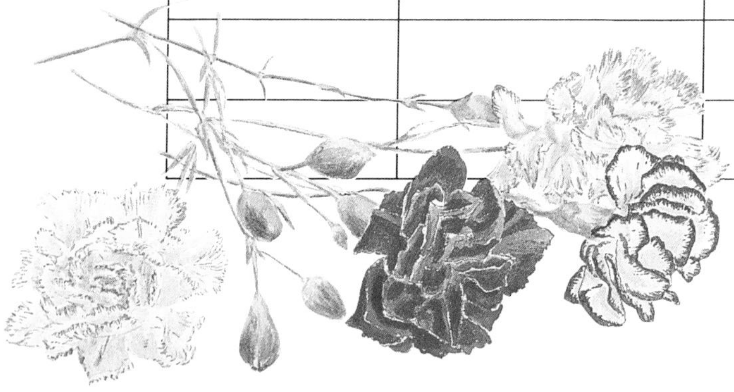

Date	Name	Address

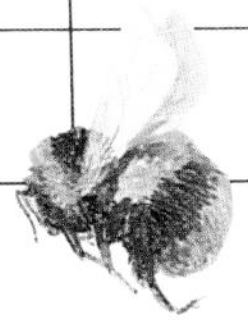

Date	*Name*	*Address*

Date	Name	Address

Date	Name	Address

Date	Name	Address

Date	Name	Address

Date	*Name*	*Address*